The Identical Dolls

The Identical Dolls

AND OTHER FOLKTALES
Compiled by the Editors
of
Highlights for Children

Compilation copyright © 1995 by Highlights for Children, Inc.
Contents copyright by Highlights for Children, Inc.
Published by Highlights for Children, Inc.
P.O. Box 18201
Columbus, Ohio 43218-0201
Printed in the United States of America

ISBN 0-87534-665-0

Highlights is a registered trademark of Highlights for Children, Inc.

CONTENTS

The Identical Dolls

An Indian Folktale

Retold by Rita Dibble

One day a wise old man came into King Akbar's court with a gift. He brought three identical dolls to present to the king. As he presented the dolls, the old man said to the king, "These dolls represent a challenge, Your Majesty. They are exactly alike—except in one very important way. I wonder if Your Majesty can discover the difference?"

Akbar looked very carefully at the dolls, but they were absolutely identical. He asked if the difference was on the inside of the dolls. The old man gave a mysterious answer to that. "To eyes that can judge, the difference is obvious."

Whenever Akbar was faced with a puzzling problem, he consulted his most trusted adviser, Birbal. Akbar told Birbal, "The old man is leaving tomorrow, and I would like a solution before that." Birbal bowed to the king and took the dolls to his home. All night he sat alone, examining the dolls. He turned them this way and that and studied them from all angles.

The next morning Birbal walked into the court smiling. He bowed to Akbar and the old man and said, "These dolls represent three types of friends. One is the type you can trust with anything, the next is one who is indifferent, and the last one is the kind who cannot be trusted. A wise monarch must be able to recognize these traits in people." The old man was satisfied. He bowed low to the king and took his leave.

When he was gone Akbar asked Birbal, "How did you find out what the dolls represented?"

Birbal smiled and replied, "It was a simple experiment, Your Majesty." He sat the dolls side by side on a table and brought out three long pieces of straw. He put the straw into an ear of the first doll and the straw disappeared. "This, Your Majesty, is a trustworthy friend. You can tell him anything and he can keep your secrets." He put a straw through one ear of the second doll, and it came out of its other ear. "This one is the indifferent person," Birbal said. "He doesn't care enough to be loyal to anything but his own interests." Then Birbal put a straw through the ear of the third doll, and it came out through its mouth. "Beware of this person," said Birbal. "He is the friend you cannot afford to have."

Akbar smiled. "You, on the other hand, are exactly the kind of friend every king needs. Thank you, Birbal."

The Spider Who Couldn't Spin

By Lee Ebler

Harold was a small spider who could not weave a web no matter how hard he tried. He tried till his eight legs ached and his body sagged. He tried until his head got shaky and his spinnerets were all spun out. Sometimes he started at the bottom of a branch and tried to go up. Other times he started at the top and tried to go down. But all he could make was a tangle. Often he got caught in the tangle, which was embarrassing.

Then the other spiders had to unravel him. That made him dizzy.

"Harold," said Willie, who made beautiful, sticky webs in the fence corner, "you're probably not even a spider. You're an old bug!"

"Am not!" said Harold.

"Old bug! Old bug!" all the other spiders sang. They stood by their neat, strong webs and laughed at him.

"I'll show you!" said Harold, and he wobbled off toward the woods. He was still a little dizzy from the last unraveling.

When Harold got to the woods, he was too sad to make a web. So he sat on a stick, tucked four of his legs under his head, and thought about how he would go hungry.

"Winter's coming," said a deep voice above him. Harold looked up and saw a beautiful orange-and-black garden spider sitting in the corner of the biggest, most well-made web he'd ever seen. The web was half in shadows, half in sunlight. It dazzled Harold's eight eyes.

"Yes," said Harold, and he felt very small. Right then he decided he would never again try to spin.

"Got to get busy," said the wonderously colored garden spider.

"Yes," said Harold again.

"Well, go ahead," said the garden spider, who liked to take charge. "Spin!"

"I can't," said Harold. "I've tried and tried. I just get tangled."

The garden spider looked at Harold as if he were a caught fly. "Something's wrong. Let's fix it. Now, let's see. What do you think about when you try to spin?"

"I worry," said Harold. "I worry about getting tangled and running out of silk. I worry about getting stuck. I worry about keeping track of all my legs, and sometimes I trip over them."

"That's your problem," said the garden spider. "You're thinking about yourself, not your web. Before a spider can spin, he has to imagine his web. He has to imagine it in moonlight and sunshine. He has to imagine it in rain and dew. Now, dream a web in your mind."

Harold closed his eight eyes and tried to dream a web. At first, all he could see was himself in a tangle. Harold sighed and tried again. Slowly a web appeared in his mind. It was a tiny web, but it was sturdy. He could almost feel it.

"All right," said the garden spider. "Now spin!"

Harold was going to say "I can't," but something came over him. He felt tingly from his pedipalps to his spinnerets. He wanted to be light and spinny and to make something where nothing was before. He wanted to swing and glide and fall and weave. He felt himself begin to move. It was easy and hard at the same time. It was wonderful!

"Web," said Harold. "Web! Web! Web! Web in moonlight and sunshine and rain. Web in dew and wind and heat and cold and shadows." And then, just as suddenly, he felt tired. He felt tired as only a spider who has been doing spider-work can feel.

"Open your eyes," said the garden spider.

Harold slowly opened his eyes. All around him was a web. True, it was a small web, and one corner was a bit lopsided, but it was sturdy. Just to be sure, Harold *plinked* on the strands. The silk gave and then snapped back in place.

"You see," said the garden spider, who also liked to point things out, "it takes both dreaming and spinning to get the job done."

"But what if I go home and can't spin?" said Harold. His eight legs felt quivery again.

"Oh, fiddlesticks!" said the garden spider impatiently. "A spider can spin anywhere, anytime. He only has to dream his web first. Now, go along. Winter's coming."

"Thank you," said Harold. He started for home, scared and hopeful. His mind was full of big webs, small webs, dewy webs, and dreamy webs.

"Web," said Harold, making a kind of song. "Web! Web! Web! Web in moonlight and sunshine and rain. Web in dew and wind. Web in heat and cold and silver shadows. My web, all snug and homey!"

From that day on, Harold was able to spin. He spun small webs because he was a small spider. But no one ever again laughed at him. No one ever again had to unravel him. He was respected, even by Willie.

And if anyone asked what he had learned in the woods, he always said, "I learned how to dream!"

Trouble

A West Indian Folktale

Retold by Vashanti Rahaman

Saki the monkey lived in a warm, green country covered with thick rain forest. People built houses and sugar mills and shops and cocoa houses there. But the great forest ruled the land, ruled the sugarcane, ruled the cocoa, and ruled the people.

Saki's mother did not like the people. She warned Saki, "Stay away from the places where people live. You will find only trouble there."

Saki tried to do as his mother had said, but even in the deep forest he could not avoid people. One morning Saki found a mango tree near a path. It was laden with ripe, juicy mangoes, so he scrambled up into the branches to pick the best one for breakfast.

He heard a noise and quickly hid in the thickest part of the tree. An old lady, carefully balancing a jar on her head, shuffled down the path.

Just as she walked under the mango tree, she stumbled and the jar fell and broke. A thick brown liquid oozed out.

"Look at my trouble! Just look at my trouble!" moaned the old lady. She sat on her heels and rocked back and forth. Finally, she fixed her head kerchief and carefully picked up the largest piece of the broken jar. It was still full of the brown liquid, and she dipped her fingers into it and licked them.

"Just look at my trouble!" she wailed again. And she went on her way, still licking her fingers.

As soon as the old lady was gone, Saki climbed down and tasted the brown liquid. It was sweet, sweeter than any fruit he had ever eaten. Soon he had licked clean every piece of broken jar.

I have never tasted anything as good as this Trouble, thought Saki. *I must find some more.*

Then Saki remembered what his mother had said. *She said that I would find Trouble at the places where people live,* he told himself as he ran down the path.

Soon he came to a village. In the yard of the first house was a stand with several jars on it. *Ah-ha!* thought Saki as he went into the yard. *Here is my Trouble!*

He jumped onto the stand, and the jars toppled with a crash. Saki looked with disappointment at the broken jars. There was no brown liquid oozing out.

To make matters worse, a woman ran out of the house, swinging a broom and yelling at Saki. She was followed by two large dogs that barked and yelped as they galloped toward him. Saki leaped over the toppled stand and fled into the forest with the dogs close on his tail.

He raced up the nearest tree, a gru-gru palm covered with prickles. "Ah yah yie!" bawled Saki. He started back down, but the dogs jumped and snarled around the bottom of the tree.

"No, dogs! Go away!" yelled Saki. He pelted the dogs with gru-gru fruit, but the dogs did not leave until it was almost sunset.

Just then a girl came running down the path, singing to herself and carrying a jar on her head. As she passed under the gru-gru palm, she stumbled, and though she tried to catch the jar, it fell to the ground and broke. A thin red liquid spilled out.

"Just look at my trouble!" cried the girl, shaking her hands in distress. "Just look at my trouble!" Then she noticed that the red liquid had splashed onto her arms, and that seemed to upset her even more. "Oh no! Look at my trouble!" she wailed. "Now I have to wash it off." She ran toward the little river nearby, holding her arms as far from the rest of her body as she could.

As soon as she was out of sight, Saki climbed down from the gru-gru palm. He picked up the largest piece of the broken jar and drank. The red stuff was like liquid fire.

"Yee-owww!" howled Saki. His mouth and stomach burned. He had never tasted anything so terrible since the day he had eaten one of those strange berries that his mother called hot peppers. Saki dashed down to the river and drank water until he could drink no more.

That night, before Saki went to sleep he told his mother, "Mama, I tasted Trouble today. At first it was sweet, and I went to look for more. But I almost got killed trying to find it. Then when I found it, it burned me."

"That is how Trouble is, my child," said his mother sadly. "That is how Trouble is."

The Trolls
in the
Mill

A Swedish Folktale

Retold by Judy Cox

Anders had been traveling all day without seeing a single soul. Already the shadows grew long and cold. Anders's feet hurt and his stomach growled with hunger. Next to him, leashed on an iron chain, Snowflake growled with hunger, too. It was time to find a meal and shelter for the night.

Anders spotted a thin wisp of smoke in the woods. "Looks like a house over there," he said, tugging on Snowflake's leash. He and the big white bear turned off the main road, following the narrow trail toward the smoke.

The smoke came from the chimney of a mill. Out front, the miller, dressed in a leather apron, was digging turnips. "Evening," said Anders. He enjoyed watching the miller's eyes widen at the sight of the white bear. "We've traveled long and hard. May we spend the night in your mill?"

The miller eyed them uneasily, but when he saw the stout chain securing the bear, he nodded. "Join me for supper as well," he added. "Few strangers pass this way."

Anders and the miller shared a pot of rabbit stew while Snowflake crunched the bones. Anders thought wistfully of how nice it must be to have a hot meal and your own bed every night.

"How come ye are traveling with a wild beast?" asked the miller.

"I've trained her from a cub, I have," said Anders. "We're off to seek our fortunes and to see the world." He played a tune on the wooden flute he carried in his knapsack, and Snowflake swayed to the music, padding in circles on her big paws.

"A dancing bear," nodded the miller. "'Tis honored, I am." He sighed with regret, for he had seen no more of the world than his own mill.

"Ye may spend the night here in my mill," he told them. "But I'll warn ye. The mill is plagued with trolls. Night after night they give me no sleep. I've tried everything I can think of to run them off, but nothing works."

"Thank you," said Anders. "We'll spend the night. Perhaps we can help you with your troubles."

Anders and Snowflake bedded down on the straw inside the mill. About midnight, three trolls came in—one so big and round the other two had to carry him. They saw Anders, but not the bear, who was sleeping soundly deep in the straw.

Anders watched as the trolls built a fire and fried their dinner. He wrinkled his nose at the stench of charred meat. One troll took a long stick and prodded him. "Eat," he grunted. But Anders shook his head. He knew better than to eat troll food. Magic food is never good for humans. The troll shrugged and the three gobbled up the feast.

Soon the trolls began to fight over the last of their food. The big one said, "Give me!" but the smaller trolls wouldn't. The big troll threw the dinner bones, and they hit Snowflake and woke her. With a growl, she leaped out of the straw and attacked the trolls. They quickly gathered up their pots and pans and dishes and fled into the night.

In the morning, the miller came by. "I heard noises in the night," he said. "How did ye sleep?"

"It was not as peaceful as a thunderstorm," said Anders. "But we managed to get a bit o' shut-eye." During the night it had snowed, and when Anders looked outside the mill door, he saw that the road was covered with heavy, wet snow. Anders asked the miller if he and Snowflake might pass another night in the mill.

The miller shrugged. "If ye wish," he said.

The trolls came at midnight, as before. But as soon as they started to enter the mill door, Anders put his lips to his wooden flute and trilled a few notes. Snowflake reared on her hind legs and let out a tremendous *ROAR!* The trolls yelped and fell back outside into the cold, wet snow.

All night they prowled about the mill, howling like the wind. "We get King Troll," shouted the big troll, shaking his fist. "He eat you in one bite! And your white kitty cat, too!"

The next day, Anders asked the miller if they might stay a third night. "Whoever starts a job must finish it," Anders told the miller. The miller, who had heard the howls and roars during the night, agreed.

That night, Anders was ready for the trolls. With the miller's help, he'd boiled up a nice big pot of tar. When King Troll came, he opened his enormous mouth. "Did you ever see such a big mouth?" the ugly troll bragged.

"Did you ever taste such hot porridge?" replied Anders, and he tipped the pot and poured the tar into the troll's mouth.

The troll hopped up and down, howling in pain. He ran outside, scooped up huge handfuls of the wet snow, and shoved them in his mouth. Then he ran off into the woods.

The other trolls stared at each other. Anders unchained Snowflake, and she rushed toward them, chasing all the trolls into the woods. "Carry me!" the round troll yelled, but the others wouldn't wait. Snowflake caught the seat of his pants as he dashed away.

In the morning, Anders and the bear left, on their way to see the world. "I hope ye find fortune," the miller told them.

The miller was not bothered by trolls for many years. But some time later, a large, round troll appeared at the mill. "Is that big white kitty cat still here?" he asked.

The miller eyed the ugly troll and scratched his head. "Why, yes," he replied cleverly. "And guess what? She's had kittens!"

The troll ran off, scared silly, and troubled the miller no more.

Eight Loaves of Bread

Adapted from the Arabic

By Vesta Condon and José Guerrero Lovillo

Once upon a time, in faraway Cordoba, there lived two poor men whose names were Casim and Muhamed. They worked together in the fields.

One noon they sat down by the road to eat. Casim had five small loaves of bread and Muhamed had three. They spread a clean cloth on the ground and put the loaves of bread on it. That was all they had to eat but they were quite content.

Just then a man passed by. "Good day, my friends," said the man politely. "May you enjoy your food."

"Thank you, good sir," answered Casim and Muhamed with equal politeness. "Please sit down and enjoy it with us."

So the man sat down on the ground beside them. Casim and Muhamed broke each of the eight loaves into three pieces and then divided them equally so that each man had eight pieces to eat.

When the man finished eating, he thanked the two friends and gave them eight gold coins, saying, "Please accept these gold coins to pay for the share of your bread." Then he went away.

But Casim and Muhamed began to quarrel over the eight gold coins.

"Five coins are for me and three for you," said Casim, "because I had five loaves of bread and you had only three."

"Not so!" cried Muhamed. "Four are for me and four are for you. That's the fair way to divide them."

Well, neither one would give in, so they quit work and went to see the Cadi, or judge. They told the Cadi about the eight loaves of bread they had shared with the stranger. They told him, too, that they could not agree on how to divide the eight gold coins the stranger had given them in return.

The Cadi listened carefully, then turned to Muhamed. "Since Casim had five loaves and you had only three, why won't you accept the three gold coins and let Casim have five?"

"Because I don't think that's fair. I think I should have just as many gold coins as Casim does."

"To be fair," said the Cadi, "you should receive one gold coin and Casim should have seven."

"How can that be?" cried Muhamed. "Why should I have only one gold coin when I don't think even three are enough?"

"Well," said the Cadi, "you broke each of the loaves into three pieces, which make twenty-four pieces altogether. You all ate the same number of pieces. Is that right?"

"Yes, that's right," answered Muhamed.

The Cadi continued. "You, Muhamed, ate eight pieces of bread, but you gave only nine, so you had just one left over. Casim, however, who also ate eight pieces, gave fifteen, so he had seven left over. Therefore, the man ate seven of Casim's pieces but only one of yours, so Casim should have seven coins and you only one. Isn't that right?"

"Yes," said Muhamed, scratching his head.

Then he took his one coin, Casim took his seven coins, and the two friends went off to work in the field together.

Happily Ever After

A Modern Folktale

By Vashanti Rahaman

One Saturday morning, not such a very long time ago, Gregory, the pediatrician's son, married a beautiful princess.

Ah, thought Gregory. *Now I shall start living happily ever after.*

And so he did, until the following Thursday. Then he lost his job at the engineering company where he worked. There were no other engineering jobs in town. So Gregory stayed home.

Things began to get rather dull.

The princess was still beautiful, of course, and things were not at all dull when she was at home. But she was away most of the day, for she was a marine biologist and studied the ocean.

So Gregory spent all of Friday looking at the job advertisements in the newspapers. He found lots of jobs that he could do if he had to—plumber's jobs, electrician's jobs, gardener's jobs, cook's jobs, manager's jobs, tutor's jobs, even baby-sitter's jobs. But there wasn't a single job that he thought he might like to do all the time.

On Friday night he said to the princess, "There aren't any jobs that seem right for me. I think I'll wait for you to become queen. Then I'll help you rule the country and all that."

"Oh, dear," said the princess, "I don't think you quite understand. I have four older brothers and sisters and they all have children. I won't ever be queen, for I am an unimportant princess."

"You are not unimportant," said Gregory. "You are very important to me."

"And you are important to me," said the princess. She smiled an especially lovely smile. "But, you see, even if I did become queen, I wouldn't rule the country. The people elect a government to do that."

"Oh," Gregory said with a sigh. "Then I shall have to find something to do soon."

The princess smiled and took his hand. "I know you will find a job that is suited especially for you!"

On Monday the princess went back to work, and Gregory was alone again. He wandered about the castle and felt sorry for himself. He sat down in dusty chairs in dusty rooms that never seemed to be used and felt even sorrier for himself. He huddled in window seats and felt sorrier still.

Finally he went back to the little living room that he and the princess used and lay down on the couch without even taking off his shoes. He was going to stay there for the rest of the day just feeling sorry for himself.

Drip! Drip! Drip! The faucet in the bathroom was dripping.

Bother, thought Gregory. *I can't feel sorry for myself properly with that faucet dripping.*

He tried to turn it off, but it kept on dripping.

So Gregory went down to the basement and found some plumber's tools. He fixed the faucet in the bathroom and the one in the kitchen and the one in the washroom off the banquet hall. He kept finding more and more dripping faucets. It took him two days to fix them all.

On Wednesday he fixed a dozen windows that wouldn't open.

On Thursday he fixed the creaky attic stairs.

On Friday and Saturday he insulated the attic. The princess helped him on Saturday.

"We need an army of people to look after this castle," said the princess. "But I'm afraid my salary isn't enough to pay an army of people."

For the next two weeks Gregory worked on the electrical system in the castle. He had to change all of the wires. It was a very old castle, and the wires were much too old to be safe.

Next, Gregory scrubbed and polished the castle. It was really quite a pretty little castle. He repaired the broken furniture and cleaned the drapes and cushions. He even cut the lawns and trimmed the shrubbery and weeded the flower and vegetable beds.

The castle took a lot of looking after.

On weekends the princess sometimes helped him, and they took turns doing the cooking and the laundry. They even found time to coach a junior soccer team.

But sometimes they just went for walks or drives in the country or picnics at the seaside.

"The castle seems more comfortable than it's ever been before," said the princess as she watched Gregory fix supper one night. She hardly ever stayed late at the laboratory anymore.

Gregory just smiled.

"Have you found a job yet?" asked the princess.

"Why, yes," said Gregory. "I've been working at my new job for weeks and weeks."

The princess thought for a while. "What job?" she asked. "You've done nothing but work here at the castle for weeks and weeks." Then suddenly she smiled. "Oh, I see! Of course!" she said. "That's it."

And they really did live happily ever after, most of the time.

Snow Quest

By J.L. Bell

"Snow," said Queen Zaleeka. She slid the word across her tongue like a sliver of melting ice. "I wonder what snow feels like."

Snowflakes never fell in the wide warm valley where Queen Zaleeka ruled. But from her terrace she could see mountaintops as white as the clouds around them. "As queen, I cannot leave my valley," she lamented. "I will never feel snow." She shook her head sadly, and her long, black braid swayed to and fro.

A young herdsman named Jabari heard of the queen's sorrow. He was strong enough to wrestle an ox to the ground and brave enough to journey to the mountains. "I will bring snow to the queen," Jabari decided.

Jabari followed the chirp of a flute to find his younger brother, Nuru. "We are going to the mountains for snow," he said.

"I will stay and look after your camels," said Nuru.

"I need all four camels, and I need someone to help," Jabari answered. "Besides, the last time I went away, you played your flute and forgot the camels. It took us three days to find them."

Nuru followed Jabari to the corral. Each brother climbed onto one camel and grabbed a rope attached to another camel's harness. They rode east. Nuru played a tune that fit the camels' rolling walk. After an hour he looked back. "Our village looks like a pile of leaves swept into the corner of the valley," he said.

The brothers reached the foot of the mountains as night fell. Jabari tied the camels to two broad trees. Nuru played a quiet melody to the stars.

"Why do you make this quest? What will you do with the snow?" Nuru asked his brother.

"I will give the snow to Queen Zaleeka," Jabari replied. "Then I will ask her to marry me."

"I hope she answers yes," Nuru replied. The brothers rolled over and slept.

In the morning Jabari untied the two camels that had not carried them the day before. The brothers rode that pair up the mountainside. "This path curls around like a snake dozing in the sun," Nuru muttered. He tried blowing his flute, but the high mountain air made him dizzy.

When the path became too narrow for the camels, Jabari took their leather saddlebags on his own shoulders. The brothers kept climbing. At last they clambered onto a shady plateau. Before them lay a broad field of snow, white and glistening, with whiskers of fog rising off its chilly surface.

"Snow for the queen!" said Jabari. He tossed Nuru one pair of saddlebags. "Help me fill these." The brothers scooped up snow with their hands. Jabari filled two bags before his brother had finished one.

"The snow glitters like the stars last night," Nuru remarked. He blew on his hands to warm them.

Frowning, Jabari filled the last bag. "Are your bags full?" he asked. Nuru nodded. "Come, then!"

The brothers dashed back down the rocky trail. Jabari jumped straight onto the camel's back. Nuru climbed onto the other, the heavy leather bags pressing on his back.

"Ride as fast as you can!" Jabari yelled. "We must reach the village before the snow melts!" The brothers raced to the base of the mountain. They saddled the fresh camels under the trees and galloped west.

Jabari howled and slapped his camel's side. Nuru clutched his camel's neck, which was slippery with dust and sweat. He felt the wind slice across his eyes. His breath popped from his lungs at every bump.

At sunset Jabari and Nuru rode into their village and straight to the queen's castle. Hearing the uproar, Zaleeka stepped outside. Her striped robe shimmered in the red sun. She smiled when she saw Jabari and Nuru. "Why do you come in such a hurry, brothers?" she asked.

"I have been to the mountains for you," announced Jabari. He hoisted the saddlebags in his hands. "I have brought you snow!"

Jabari opened all four bags and turned them over. Water poured out onto the grass at the queen's feet. In the center of the puddle was a ball of gray slush, no bigger than an egg.

Queen Zaleeka sighed. "That is not how I imagined snow."

Jabari gasped, then hung his head in embarrassment. "The camels' warm bodies must have melted it," he said.

"I so wanted to feel snow," said the queen. Nuru watched her turn away from his brother.

"Wait!" Nuru stepped forward. "Imagine cloud-white snow covering the ground thicker than banana leaves in the fall."

Queen Zaleeka closed her eyes. In a moment she said, "I can see it."

"Pick up the snow in your hands. First it is like flour dough that you can squeeze into a ball. Then it feels like sharp teeth biting your fingers. But after a minute the snow turns into cold water and runs down your arms, making a shiny trail of goose bumps."

"I can feel it," said Queen Zaleeka, shivering. She opened her eyes and smiled a dazzling smile. "Nuru, your words have brought snow to me. What do you wish in return?"

Nuru's face grew warm. "I would never have left the village and seen snow if Jabari had not taken me to the mountains. He is a brave man who loves you greatly. I wish to play my flute at the ceremony of your marriage . . . to my brother."

"So you shall," said the queen. And she smiled at Jabari with teeth as white as snow.

The Moonfish

By Caroline Stutson

It was dark when Sago parted the reeds that grew along the river and set out on his journey. For it was the custom of his people, on the eve of their tenth birthdays, to go where the river met the sea. They went to search for moonfish.

In the distance, he could hear the gentle pounding of the mighty ocean waves. As long as he could remember, he had fished the shores there, but never at night. Never alone.

Suddenly, something slithered across the path! Sago jumped back, his heart beating wildly.

"It is only Black Snake on her way to somewhere else," he reasoned, catching his breath and hurrying on down the trail.

At the top of the cliff, Sago looked back. He was not certain, but it seemed to him that someone was watching.

"Perhaps it is a river spirit," he whispered, "a spirit that wishes me to leave this place."

Then, just as the moon slipped from behind a cloud, he saw it—a silver flash of a face hovering above the reeds!

"Sago?" a voice called softly.

It was Marobi! But why had she come to the shore? Didn't his older sister trust him enough to search for the moonfish?

"Sago, please don't be angry." Marobi stepped out of the tall grass. "I have brought you a gift from the ocean."

With a sigh, Sago sank down on the cliff. He had used most of his courage to come this far. Now it would be all too easy to return with her before the search had begun. But he said nothing.

Marobi handed him the gift. It was a small, brittle starfish. Five perfect arms pointed from a star within.

"There's a story, too," she said, sitting beside him.

Sago stared at the ocean. Perhaps if he did not reply, his sister might go away.

"Long, long ago," began Marobi, "a Star Child lived in the sky with his brothers and sister. But it was not enough for him to see Earth from the sky every evening. The Star Child wanted to know more.

"Night after night he begged his sister, the Moon, 'If only you would ask our father, the Sun, to let me stay until day comes, then I could see what the world is really like.'

"At last, the Moon agreed to do as he requested."

"What did the Sun father say?" questioned Sago, who was listening closely in spite of himself.

Marobi went on with the story. "The Sun would not allow it. He told the Moon to tell Star Child:

The Sun alone must glow by day,
And in the night, the stars must stay!'

"Oh, Star Child was most unhappy with his father's answer." Marobi smiled at her brother, who was tracing the arms of the starfish with one finger.

"The Sun alone must glow by day, and in the night, the stars must stay," repeated Sago. "Did Star Child obey his father?" he asked.

"What do you think?"

"He did what he wanted without permission."

45

"It is so. One night, when all of his brothers and his sister had left the sky, the Star Child stayed to see what the world was like by day."

"Was he punished for it?"

"Never again could he shine at night with his brothers and sister, and Star Child dropped down into the sea and . . ."

"Turned into a starfish like this," finished Sago.

His sister laughed. "Yes! But you know I think the Sun was sorry afterward. For he loved his little Star Child."

Sago rubbed the starfish his sister had given him. He was certain now that it would bring him luck. He was glad that Marobi had stayed to talk with him.

"Starfish grow their arms back when they have broken," he said. "Did the Sun give them that power because he was sad about what happened to Star Child?"

Marobi stood and brushed the sand from her dress. "That I do not know," she answered, "but this is why I have given it to you. It's to help you find the moonfish as it once helped me."

Sago jumped up. "Something is wrong with that story," he told his sister. "Didn't Star Child's father say that the Sun alone must glow by day, and in the night, the stars must stay? But many times, I have seen the Moon in the daytime. Why is that?" he demanded.

"Because," Marobi called as she disappeared among the river reeds, "sometimes big sisters must check on their younger brothers, whether they like it or not!"

The Six Sillies

An Old English Tale

Retold by Josepha Sherman

Once upon a time six silly friends went for a walk. Their names were Bill and Jill, Ann and Dan, and Sam and Pam. They came to a little river and waded across. But when they had reached the other side of the river, Bill said, "Did we all cross the river? Are we all here?"

"I don't know," said Ann.

"We had better count ourselves to be sure," said Sam. "One, two, three, four, five. Oh no! I counted only five! There should be six of us!"

"Let me count," Pam said. "One, two, three, four, five. It's true! I counted only five, too!"

Jill counted. Ann counted. Bill and Dan counted. They all counted, "One, two, three, four, five!"

"Oh no!" the sillies cried. "One of us is missing! One of us must have fallen in the river and drowned! Oh no, oh no!"

A traveler came riding by. He heard the six sillies. "What is wrong?" he asked.

"We went for a walk," said Bill.

"And now one of us is gone," added Ann.

"One of us must have drowned in the river!" cried Jill.

"But that river is very shallow," the traveler said. "No one could drown in it. How many of you were there at the start?"

"There were six," Sam told him.

"But there are still six," said the traveler.

"No, no. We all counted. There are only five!"

The traveler got down from his horse. "Show me how you counted," he said.

Sam pointed to the other sillies. "One, two, three, four, five."

"Poor sillies," the traveler said, smiling. "Look." He counted them, tapping each one on the head as he counted. "One, two, three, four, five, six. See?"

"Six!" the sillies cried. "You've found our friend!"

"No, no, no!" said the traveler. "Your friend was never missing. When you counted heads, you each forgot to count your own. That is how you counted only five, not six."

Shaking his head, the traveler got back on his horse and rode away. The six sillies looked at each other.

"How could that be?" Bill asked. He counted again. "One, two, three, four, five. Oh no! The traveler must have made our friend disappear again!" he whined.

"But—but that must mean he is a wizard!" cried Ann.

"A wizard!" cried the six sillies. They ran back to their village as fast as they could. "Help!" they shouted. "How many of us are there?"

"Why, there are six of you," said a woman in the village.

Six! The sillies smiled at each other.

"The wizard must have given us back our missing friend," said Bill. "But which one of us was it? Which one was missing?"

They tried and tried, but nobody could remember being missing. At last the sun went down and the moon came up. But the six silly friends never did figure out what happened.

The Vulture
and the
Rain God

An African Folktale

Retold by Bonnie Highsmith Taylor

In the beginning there was a time when no rain fell. For months and months it did not rain a drop.

The earth turned brown. All the plants and the grass withered and died. All the animals, and there were only animals in the beginning, were starving. Many died from thirst.

Lord Lion raised his head to the skies and cried, "Oh, God of Rain, send down water to the earth."

But the Rain God did not answer.

Then Elephant called out, "Oh, mighty Mighty One who is the most powerful of all the gods, please send us rain."

Still the Rain God did not answer.

Monkey climbed to the top of a kapok tree and screeched, "Please, don't let us die! We will do anything you ask if you will only send rain."

In a booming voice that crackled the parched earth, the Rain God answered. "Bring me gifts of riches and you shall have rain."

The animals all cheered.

"We will send emeralds," said Lord Lion.

"And pearls," said Elephant.

Monkey climbed down from the kapok tree. "And moonstones," he said.

The gifts were gathered together and tied in a silk kerchief.

Hedgehog stepped forward. "We must decide which bird will carry the gifts to the Rain God."

"Owl," said Lord Lion. "He is strong and fast."

"But it is a long journey," said Owl. "I do not fly well in the daytime."

Parakeet was chosen.

"But with my short, stubby beak," he said, "I would have trouble carrying the bundle."

Flamingo refused, saying, "I will not mess up my beautiful plumage."

At last Vulture said, "Give me the bundle, and I will take it to the Rain God."

The animals thought Vulture was too large and clumsy to fly so far. But all the other birds refused.

In those times Vulture's beak was long and straight. He lifted the kerchief in his beak and began his journey.

On and on he flew. Higher and higher.

The hot sun beat down on Vulture's head. His body ached. But on he went until, at last, he reached the kingdom of the Rain God.

Vulture had no sooner dropped the bundle and started back down to earth than the heavy rains began. By the time he reached the ground the grass and the plants were turning green.

But poor Vulture!

The sun had badly burned the top of his head. All the feathers had fallen out.

His long, straight beak had melted and was now a curved lump. From that day forward he was unable to hunt for food. Now he eats only what others have left behind.

But though Vulture is a rather ugly bird today, he was once so brave that he saved the lives of all the animals in the world.

How
Pecos Bill
Got His Name
and Then
Got Famous

By Betty Bates

Out in the Wild West, they tell the tale of a cowboy so tall he had to climb a ladder to shave. They tell of the fellow who killed a poisonous snake by putting its tail in its mouth so it swallowed itself. And they also tell the story of Pecos Bill.

They say that Bill was born in east Texas, in a house crowded with a horse, a cow, chickens, pigs, his ma, his pa, and his sixteen older brothers and sisters. Once in a while, when Bill brought home one of his playmates—a bear, or maybe a mountain lion—the family would make an extra place at the table for it.

One day, when Bill had grown to maybe a year old, a new family moved in. That is, they settled about fifty miles down the river. "Them folks is too close," said Bill's pa. "We're leavin'."

So, since they couldn't have the place to themselves, Bill's folks packed up the cow, chickens, pigs, and seventeen children and headed west in a wagon pulled by the horse.

As they neared the Pecos River, Bill fell out of the wagon. Of course, being part of such a big family, he wasn't missed for weeks. His folks were surely surprised when they found him gone, but what could they do?

Meanwhile, Bill had met up with the chief of the coyotes, who lived in the hills neighboring the Pecos River. It wasn't long before Bill had been adopted by the coyotes, and there he stayed. As he grew up, he learned the coyote language and learned to yelp like a coyote at night. So, naturally, he thought he was a coyote.

One morning, Bill was sitting down to his breakfast of bear meat when a cowboy called Waco Jones rode up. He gave Bill a long look. "How come you're running around among all these varmints?"

"Can't you see I am a varmint?" said Bill. "I'm a Texas coyote."

Waco Jones leaned back in his saddle and let out a loud guffaw.

"Somethin' funny?" asked Bill.

An hour later, when Waco had recovered from his laughing spell, he said, "Bust my britches, you ain't no coyote."

"All I know," said Bill, "is that I got fleas. Besides, I howl all night, like any ordinary coyote."

"Ain't no Texans without fleas," said Waco, "and most of us are howlers. Lookee here, did you ever see a coyote without a tail? Well, where's your tail?"

Bill looked very carefully. "Durned if you ain't right. I never noticed that."

"You're a human," said Waco.

"Reckon so," said Bill, "whatever that may be. Guess I'll join up with you humans."

Bill turned to Chief Coyote. "I thank you kindly for your hospitality, but it's time for me to move along," he said.

"If you must, you must," yelped the chief. "Drop us a line now and then."

Bill nodded, took a last bite of bear meat, jumped up behind Waco's saddle, and howled good-bye to his friends the coyotes.

"What's your name?" asked Waco.

"Name?" said Bill. "Bless me if I know. But now that I think of it, I seem to remember my folks calling me Bill."

"That all?"

"Ain't that enough?"

"Nope," said Waco. "You gotta have a last name."

The Pecos River lay spread out ahead of them. "How about Pecos River Bill?" said Bill.

"Too long," said Waco. "Not snappy enough."

"Well, how about just Pecos Bill?"

Waco shook his head. "You got the names twisted around."

"In that case my last name'll be first. Pecos Bill's got a ring to it, and since I spent the best part of my life in these parts, I'll take it."

That's how Pecos Bill got his name.

He thrived among the humans. Since there are so many yarns about him going here and going there, he surely met up with a long lost brother or sister at one time or another. Maybe he met up with all sixteen siblings. He raised his horse Widow-Maker on nitroglycerin and dynamite, and it bucked off everybody but him. He acquired a squatter-hound called Norther to help him hunt buffalo. And he fell for a pretty girl named Slue-Foot Sue, who rode a catfish bigger than a whale down the Rio Grande.

They say Bill did away with all the bad men in west Texas. They say he had a rope as long as the equator and could rope a whole herd of cattle with it. They say he fought a three-ton mountain lion and rode it down a canyon, whooping and hollering, a hundred feet at a jump. They say he once rode a cyclone. And they say he dug the Grand Canyon single-handed.

That's how Pecos Bill got his name and then got famous.

Squirrel Saves the Sun

Adapted from a Native American Folktale

By Marianne Mitchell

One morning, a long time ago, the sun did not come up. In the long, dark night the owl and the wolf kept right on hunting. Snug inside their holes, the rabbits and chipmunks kept right on sleeping.

But after a while, the owl and wolf were tired of hunting. "When will Sun come up so we can get some rest?" they asked each other. "It should be morning by now."

Even the rabbits and chipmunks finally woke up. "We're hungry. Isn't it time for us to go to breakfast?" they asked each other. They looked at the sky. "Why isn't Sun up yet?"

Finally, all the animals were sure that something was very wrong. They all came together in a clearing in the woods. Everyone had an idea about what had happened to Sun.

"Maybe he forgot to wake up," said Bear.

"He wouldn't dare forget such an important job," said Owl.

"We have to find him," said Eagle. "If it is night forever, we will be cold and hungry."

"Maybe he's hiding," said Rabbit. So Rabbit and all the animals that were good at burrowing in holes went off to look for Sun.

"Maybe he's lost," said Wolf. So Wolf and all the animals who had good noses went sniffing through the forest in search of Sun.

"I think he is caught in the branches of a tree," said Squirrel. So all the birds with sharp eyes flew off in every direction to look for Sun.

Squirrel wished he could fly, too. But he did the best he could by leaping from branch to branch, looking for Sun in the treetops. After he had traveled a long, long way, he noticed that the sky was just a tiny bit lighter.

"I'm getting close!" cried Squirrel. He scampered even faster toward the light.

Soon he came to a huge oak tree with branches that reached to the sky. There, stuck in the very top, was Sun. He was pale and weak as he called out to Squirrel.

"Help me, Squirrel!" cried Sun. "I was so foolish this morning. I flew too close to the earth. Now I am caught in this tree. The longer I am here, the weaker I get."

Squirrel wasted no time and hurried up the big tree. But the closer he got to Sun, the hotter it became. He nibbled on the branches that were holding Sun. Slowly, Sun started to rise a bit. He grew brighter and hotter.

"Whew! It's getting very hot near you, Father Sun," said Squirrel.

"Don't worry," said Sun. "Chew some more and soon I will be free."

Squirrel chewed a few more branches. Sun rose a little more. He grew brighter and hotter—so hot that Squirrel's soft brown fur sizzled and turned black.

"Oh no! Look what happened to my fur!" cried Squirrel. "I can't chew anymore, Father Sun. It's too hot for me."

"But you must! If I stay stuck in this tree, it will be night forever. You don't want that, do you?"

Squirrel remembered how long and dark the night had been. He chewed some more. The branch bent and Sun rose a little higher. Sun glowed brighter and hotter, too—so hot that Squirrel's tail burned right off.

"Look at my beautiful tail!" cried Squirrel. "I can't chew anymore. You are too hot!"

"Please, Squirrel. Soon I will be free. Soon I can bring light and warmth to all the world."

Squirrel didn't want his friends to be cold or hungry. He didn't want it always to be night in the world. So, in spite of the awful heat, he crept a little closer to Sun. He chewed until the last branch broke and Sun was free. Sun rose high in the sky, full of his light and power.

But now Squirrel was stuck at the top of the tree. He rubbed his eyes, but couldn't see a thing. "Oh no! Your light was too strong for me. Now I am blind!"

Sun looked down on the poor creature in the tree. "Thank you, Squirrel, for saving me. It hurts me to see that your fur was burned, your tail was lost, and now you are blind. You gave up a lot to help me. For all that, I will give you anything you wish."

Squirrel huddled on his branch and thought for a moment. "I have always wished I could fly like the birds," he said.

"And so it will be," said Sun. "You will fly better than the birds, even though you are blind. Your sharp ears will guide you. You will hunt at night and sleep in the day so my bright light won't harm you again."

With that, Squirrel stretched his arms and legs. New leathery wings spread out from his dark body. He leaped into the air and flew for the first time. He called out in happiness, and the echo of his call came bouncing back to him. In this way, he knew where the rocks and trees were. He was happy to have helped Sun. And he was happy to be this new creature—the bat.

* * *

Editors' note: This folktale is based on the widely told myth that bats are blind. In fact, all bats can see. And many have good vision.

Savitri

An Indian Tale

Retold by Rita Dibble

A very long time ago, India was governed by a good and wise ruler. Not all rulers were as good. The kingdom next door was ruled by an ambitious and wicked man who had blinded and exiled the real monarch of the land. This made the good king even more determined to set an example, and his subjects were content and prosperous.

The king had one child, a lovely daughter. The princess was called Savitri. As Savitri grew, many teachers came to instruct her in mathematics, astronomy, cooking, reading, history, and writing, as well as hunting. Her father taught her to think and behave like a great ruler.

When Savitri was old enough to marry, she decided she would choose her own husband. Many monarchs and nobles came to woo her, but no one could equal her knowledge and skills.

One day after a long hunt, the royal party was returning to the palace when Savitri spotted a woodcutter in the forest. She stopped her chariot and asked the young man his name. "Satyawan, Your Highness," came the answer. Savitri was enchanted by the quiet strength of this young man. They talked for hours.

That night she saw Satyawan in her dreams, and the next day she told her father she had decided to marry him. The king was delighted, for he had recognized Satyawan as the son of the deposed and blind neighboring ruler. He arranged to have Satyawan visit the palace.

The royal court heartily approved of the princess's choice. Everyone seemed very happy, except for Savitri's old teacher, who was also the court astrologer. The princess saw her teacher grow thoughtful. After Satyawan had left, Savitri asked her teacher if something was troubling him.

The old man looked long at the princess and said, "I trust your judgment in people, Your Highness, but when the young man walked in, I saw the shadow of death over his head. He will live for another year. If you marry him, you will soon be a widow," he said.

"I will not let my husband die," said the brave princess. "Perhaps I can persuade Yama, the lord of death, to spare Satyawan."

"You have my blessings, Your Highness," said her teacher. "Just remember that Yama isn't easy to persuade."

Satyawan and Savitri were married right away. With each passing day they discovered how perfectly matched they were. But the princess was all too aware of the passage of time. She dreaded the day she would face Yama. Meanwhile, Satyawan was blissfully unaware of the shadow over him.

Finally the day arrived. It was exactly one year from the day Satyawan and Savitri had first met. Savitri resolved to stay close by Satyawan that day, to catch Yama when he came.

Around midday, Satyawan stopped to take a break from his work. He sat under the cool shade of a banyan tree and closed his eyes. Savitri sat and watched as Satyawan sighed and then stopped breathing.

The next moment she saw a dark shadow bend over Satyawan's body, and she knew Yama had arrived. Savitri bowed respectfully to Yama and said, "Please don't take him away."

Yama revealed himself to her and said kindly, "I know how you feel, child, but your husband now belongs among the dead."

Savitri stood up and said in a determined voice, "I promised to be by his side, so I will follow you."

Yama laughed and replied, "You'll soon get tired. No mortal can walk as far as the underworld." So he set off.

Behind him Yama could hear the steady jingling sound of Savitri's ankle bracelets. After a few hours, he stopped.

"Go home. This is a futile journey," he said.

"I can't go home empty-handed," said Savitri. "No one will believe I met the lord of death."

"All right, you may have anything you wish. But you cannot ask for your husband's life."

"Please grant that my father-in-law may have his eyesight restored," Savitri asked.

"Done!" said Yama. "Now go home." And he turned and continued walking.

A few minutes later he heard the familiar *jingle, jingle* and stopped again. "You are still with me?" he asked, surprised.

"Could I have one more wish? Please, your lordship," asked Savitri.

Yama's patience was wearing thin, but he was impressed by Savitri's courage and persistence. "All right," he answered. "You may have one more. But remember—you can't have Satyawan."

"Please grant that my father-in-law gets his kingdom back," Savitri said.

"Done! Now turn around and go home," Yama said. He turned and walked away.

Jingle, jingle, jingle went the bracelets behind Yama. He started to lose his temper. "What more can your father-in-law want?" he said angrily.

"Grandsons," muttered Savitri in a meek voice.

"DONE! Now stop following me." Yama turned and walked quickly away.

After a while Yama realized that he could still hear Savitri's bracelets. Now he was furious. He stopped and whirled around. There she was, two steps behind him.

"WHAT NOW?" Yama thundered.

Savitri gathered up all her courage and replied, "How can my father-in-law have grandsons if he has no son?"

Yama was furious, but he could not argue with her logic. With a final howl, Yama disappeared.

Savitri rejoiced.

Savitri and Satyawan found themselves back in the field, under the tree. They came home to a restored kingdom and lived and ruled happily together for many years.

Easy Come, Easy Go

A West Indian Folktale

Retold by Vashanti Rahaman

Small Monkey found the mango tree in the middle of the dry season. It was the only mango tree on the little island, and so well hidden that he was sure that no other monkey would find it. He danced around and jumped up and down and chattered with excitement. "You will be mine, mine alone," he said to the tree. "There will be no big monkeys around to take your mangoes from me." Then he danced around some more.

A harsh voice broke in on his celebration. "Foolish creature," it said. "Only the birds of the air will be able to reach these mangoes, and only to them will these mangoes belong."

Small Monkey looked up and saw a gloriously colored parrot sitting at the top of the tree. "Pompous windbag," he called out to the parrot. "If the birds can reach the mangoes, I can, too." That was the way to talk to parrots.

But the parrot only laughed. "You will remember my words when the rains come," he cried. Then he spread his wings and flew over the wide, wide river and into the forest.

It was time for Small Monkey to go back to his home in the forest, too. He went down to the water's edge and crossed the river at the shallow place he had found.

How clever he had been to find that shallow place! Now that he had found the mango tree, he would stay away until the rains came. He did not want anyone else to find out about the tree before the mangoes were ripe.

The hot days dragged on. Often the monkeys would go to the river to cool off. They were safe from the caimans in the dry season. During the day the big reptiles slept in the cool mud at the bottom of the deepest parts of the wide, wide river.

Sometimes one of the other monkeys would look at the little island in the middle of the river and wish out loud that there were some way to get there. How important Small Monkey would become if he told of his discovery! But he thought of the ripening mangoes and hugged his secret to himself.

Finally the rains came. For days it poured, and the monkeys huddled miserably in whatever shelter they could find. But Small Monkey was excited. Surely, some of his mangoes would be ripe now!

When the rains finally stopped and Small Monkey went down to the river, he could not find his shallow crossing place. It had disappeared! Again and again he waded into the water where the shallow place had been. Every time Small Monkey tried, the water got too deep.

He had waded out one last time when he found himself face-to-face with the most enormous caiman he had ever seen. Small Monkey had never been so terrified in his life.

How stupid of me to forget the caimans, he thought frantically.

"G-g-greetings, mighty one," said Small Monkey, trying to bow and getting a face full of water in the process. Was that the way you spoke to caimans? Small Monkey didn't know. He had never heard of anyone speaking to caimans before. He didn't even know if caimans could speak.

But he found out soon enough. "What a well-brought-up child you are," said the caiman in a most friendly and sing-songy sort of voice. "Your ma and pa have you well trained. I like to see that. Most children these days have no manners at all, no manners at all. They see an old caiman and they just bawl and run.

"But you are different. You just came up to me and said, 'Greetings,' nice and polite. So, what can I do for you?"

"Do for me, sir?" asked Small Monkey. This caiman didn't seem like a bad sort after all. Maybe, when they were not hungry, caimans were like everyone else. He hoped so.

"It seemed like you were looking for something," said the caiman. "Maybe I could help you."

"Well," said Small Monkey, "I was trying to find the shallow place to get to the island. It was here in the dry season, but it is gone now."

"And it is going to stay gone until the next dry season comes," said the caiman. "But if you want to reach the island, all you have to do is climb upon my back and I'll carry you there."

"Really?" cried Small Monkey, thinking of the ripe mangoes. "Oh, thank you, sir!" He climbed onto the caiman's broad back and held on tightly.

Soon they were far from shore, and the caiman was gently humming to himself. *This is fun,* thought Small Monkey. *The other monkeys would never believe this.*

Then the caiman began to sing.

At first, Small Monkey paid no attention to the singing. Then he noticed the words of the song:

"Come, let we go, where the Caiman Granny
  be there.
She take your head and throw it away.
Then she boil your liver for soup.
Come, let we go . . ."

Small Monkey had heard enough. Maybe the big caiman had eaten, but he had a hungry granny waiting for monkey liver. Small Monkey had to think fast.

"Soup, Mr. Caiman," he said out loud, "that sounds good." Small Monkey was thinking so fast his head hurt and he could hardly breathe.

"Yes, child," said the caiman, "that granny of mine does make the best monkey liver soup in the world. She chops it up fine and seasons it good and boils it up with a big pepper and some chive and tomato and okra."

79

Small Monkey swallowed hard and said in his most surprised-sounding voice, "Liver? All you wanted was my liver? Why didn't you tell me that at first? Now we have to go back."

"What do you mean?" asked the caiman. "You must have your liver with you. Where else could it possibly be?"

"You don't know about monkeys," said Small Monkey, thinking furiously. "We don't have hard waterproof skin like you. With all this rain, I got soaked right through. I had to take off my skin and take out my insides and squeeze out all the water. But I couldn't squeeze out my liver well enough, so I hung it on a tree back there to dry out. So if you just take me back where you found me, I'll run up the tree and get it for you."

"Well, I never," said the caiman. "You learn something new every day. What are we waiting for?"

He turned around so fast that Small Monkey had to hang on for dear life. Then they took off for the shore in a burst of speed, throwing up the water in a huge wave behind them.

The old caiman went right up onto the bank of the river. "Jump off fast, child, and get the liver," he said with a smile.

But Small Monkey had already reached the nearest tree. Quickly he climbed to the highest branches.

"What's taking you so long?" the caiman called.

"I'm thinking," Small Monkey called back.

"About what?" asked the caiman.

"About how easy it was to trick you," said Small Monkey. "You actually believed that silly story about me taking off my skin!" And he laughed long and hard.

The caiman glared up at the monkey and snapped his jaws angrily, his rows of teeth gleaming. Then he turned and slipped back into the water. "Easy come, easy go," Small Monkey heard him muttering. "There will be other monkeys. When I find them, things will be different!"

Now then, thought Small Monkey. *What was I doing before this unpleasantness? Oh no! My mangoes! I must get some.*

From his high perch he could see the tiny island across the water. There in the center of the island was his mango tree. But now it seemed to be covered with multicolored flowers.

With a sigh, Small Monkey saw that they were not flowers. They were birds. The parrot had been right after all.

For a long time Small Monkey just sat in the treetop and looked longingly at his mango tree. Then he carefully swung over into the branches of the next tree, and the next.

Easy come, easy go, thought Small Monkey as he made his way back home. *There will be other mango trees. When I find them, things will be different!*

To Catch Smoke

A Swedish Folktale

Retold by Judy Cox

Nils watched sadly as his farmhand stuffed clothes into his knapsack. "No," Tom said, without raising his eyes to Nils, "I'll not stay another day. Bumps in the night. Bangings and clankings. Cows milked when they shouldn't be. Pigs fed when there's nobody there. It's not natural." He swung his pack over his shoulder and took off down the narrow dirt road.

Nils sighed. He'd not been able to keep any help on the farm for months now, ever since the tomtar moved in. Not that he needed the help—the tomtar did all the work. But he certainly would like some company.

On his farm, Nils had cows (three) and chickens (twenty-five). He owned goats (five nannies and one billy) and a white sow named Brunhilde. He didn't know how many tomtar he had on the farm, because he never saw them.

Every country has its own household spirits—little invisible creatures who help with the work of the place. Scotland has brownies, and England has hobthrusts. Sweden has the tomtar.

With his tomtar to work the land and tend the livestock, Nils became a rich man. But he was lonely. Nils decided it was time to marry.

In the town where Nils took his produce to market there lived a pretty maid named Brigitta. Brigitta had hair like milkweed thistledown and eyes as blue as cornflowers. She had broad shoulders and strong hands for milking and spinning. And she had a soft voice. *Just right,* thought Nils, *for crooning lullabies to babies.*

Nils often hung about the market stall where Brigitta sold the tasty gooseberry pies she baked. He was not the only bachelor to sigh over Brigitta, however. Many young men wished to marry her. But Nils felt confident she would choose him. From his new, pressed trousers to the gold pocket watch he wore on a chain, Nils was the picture of wealth and prosperity.

But Brigitta would have nothing to do with him. "I like Nils well, indeed," she told her friend, Katrina. "Young and handsome and rich, too. But who knows what goes on at that farm of his? It's uncanny for one man alone to do all the work so well. People say it's haunted. I won't live with ghosts."

Nils was torn. He wanted the tomtar on the farm—for without their help, he would soon be poor again. But he wanted Brigitta to be his wife as well. The more he asked her to wed, the more she turned him down. "Get rid of the tomtar," she told him. "And we shall see what we shall see."

Then one day the tomtar finished all the work of the farm. All the animals were fed. The house was tidy, top to bottom. The garden was weeded, the fields lush and green with ripening crops. There was not another single, solitary task left to do.

Now, it is very unlucky for tomtar to be without work, for having nothing to do, they soon turn to mischief. They curdled the butter in the churn. They pinched poor Brunhilde to make her squeal.

The chickens wouldn't lay and the cows wouldn't give milk.

Nils knew it was time to get rid of the tomtar, so he set out to make more work, hoping the tomtar would get tired and leave. He bought more land. The tomtar happily plowed acres of fields. He bought more cows. They milked eight times as many cows and churned vats of butter. Nils was becoming richer and richer. The wealthier he got, the louder Brigitta said, "No."

As a last resort, he decided to have the tomtar build a road from his farm to town. Usually, Nils had to walk around a vast, bottomless swamp. He would set the tomtar to build a road through it. *They'll never finish a task the size of that*, thought Nils. *They'll give up and go away. Then I shall have my bride.*

But even as he pointed out where the road was to go, the tomtar built it before his eyes. He watched in amazement as trees were felled and sawed, and boards laid down across the swamp. Before he could blink, the sturdiest road he ever saw stretched across the swamp to town.

He slumped down on a fallen log, defeated. Forlornly, he watched the smoke from the chimney drift away in blue spirals. The tomtar would never leave. Brigitta would never marry him. Unless . . .

He smiled. "Come here," he ordered the tomtar. Even though he couldn't see them, small rustlings told him they were near. "Bring the smoke of my chimney back to me." Nils knew even the tomtar could not do that.

There was a rushing, like the passing of many small bodies through the bushes, and Nils knew he was alone.

The very next day he married Brigitta. They lived together on the farm. They were not so rich as before, and they certainly worked harder. But the work and their love kept them busy and happy.

The tomtar seemed gone for good, but after Nils and Brigitta had been married about seven years, one of the tomtar did come back, bringing a quill of thin blue smoke. Nils and Brigitta were delighted, for it would be nice to have a bit of help around the farm. The tomtar didn't cause much trouble, being a quiet sort, so they kept him on to feed the chickens and churn the butter. None of the others ever returned.

The Legend of the
Talking Grass

A Native American Story

Retold by Bonnie Highsmith Taylor

Long ago there was a valley where the grass grew green and tall. And the grass talked. It talked to the trees and the clouds and the dew-drops that awakened it in the morning. It talked to the creatures that lived in the valley.

Foxes and coyotes brought their little ones to roll and play in the cool morning grass. Little brown snakes hid from the hot afternoon sun in the shade of the grass. Rabbits and deer came every evening to nibble the tender tops of the grass. They were always careful not to harm the roots.

The talking grass was a friend to all the wild creatures. It warned them of danger. When the four winds brought news to the valley, the grass passed it on to the animals. If a storm was on the way the talking grass would tell the animals and they would take cover. When the great eagle came from the faraway mountains and circled overhead the grass would cry, "Hide! Hide!"

The field mice would dart down holes. Frogs would dive to the bottom of pools. Quail would stand like statues in the tall grass. And the eagle would fly back to the faraway mountains.

One day the east wind called out to the grass, "Danger! Hunters are coming! Warn the wild ones!" The grass whispered to the butterflies, and off they flew to tell the animals of the danger.

Closer and closer came the band of hunters carrying bows and arrows, spears and knives. When they reached the green valley they stopped and listened. They heard the grass talking to the wild creatures and to the butterflies that carried the message on and on.

The hunters were angry. They stomped and pounded the ground. "The grass has warned the creatures of our coming!" they roared.

The hunters searched and searched. Though they could see tracks going in all directions, not an animal could be found.

All day long the hunters waited, but the animals stayed hidden. When night fell, the hunters made camp in a grove of trees. They ate their supper, then lay on their blankets.

The grass heard the leader of the hunters say, "In the morning we will tear up the grass by the roots. We will destroy every blade. Then it will talk no more."

The grass trembled in the night air.

What would happen to its friends? Who would warn them of danger? They would all be killed, and the talking grass could not save them.

But the talking grass was not the only one who had heard the hunter's threat. Old Badger's den was close to their camp. It was so close that he could feel the heat from their campfire.

How his heart ached at the thought of losing his dear friend, the talking grass. But what could he do? A badger was no match against a band of mighty hunters.

Suddenly Old Badger remembered something. Once he had seen lightning strike a black stone he had dug up when making his den. The black stone had flamed for hours, then became ashes.

Silently Old Badger crept from his den.

First he stopped at the hollow log where the fox family lived. Next he went to the tree stump where he roused the rabbits and their children. Through the night he traveled on and on, from den to den.

Before daybreak all the wild creatures had made a wide circle of black stones around the green valley. Then Old Badger sneaked into the hunters' camp, pulled a burning limb from the campfire, and touched it to the ring of black coal.

When the hunters woke, they were startled at the sight before them. There was a ring of fire around the valley. They had never seen stones burn before. In terror they fled from the area and never returned.

By the end of the day the coals had turned to ashes. The valley was unharmed.

If you should ever walk through the valley, listen very closely. You may hear the grass whisper, "Hide! Hide! Someone is coming!" And the animals will hide and peek out at you as you pass by.

Marigold's Incredible Hat

By Anne Schraff

Everyone in town was getting ready for the fair. There would be prizes for the best jellies and for the handsomest sheep and pigs. There was also a prize for the best ladies' hat.

Marigold always won the prize for the best hat, and she was possessive of this honor. She could not imagine anybody else winning the prize. But this year another lady, Luella, was making a most beautiful hat. Marigold was furious when she heard that Luella was trying to win the prize.

In the dark of night Marigold crept to Luella's house. She peered in to see how Luella's hat was progressing. Marigold saw her put a huge pink bow on the front of her hat. So Marigold rushed home and made sure her hat had *two* huge pink bows.

The next night, Marigold peeked into Luella's window and watched her perch a brilliant yellow cloth canary on her hat. Marigold ran home and glued *two* canaries on her hat. When Marigold saw Luella arrange six bunches of delicate white paper flowers on her hat, she rushed home and did the same—and added six bunches of blue flowers for good measure.

At last it was the day of the fair. All the townspeople made their way toward the fairgrounds. Marigold couldn't wait to see Luella's hat. She feared Luella had added something else during the night.

When Marigold saw Luella, she cried, "Oh no!" Proudly displayed in the center of Luella's hat was an exquisite bird's nest made from little twigs. Inside it were six delicate blue-and-green glass eggs. Luella's hat was now more spectacular than Marigold's hat!

In desperation, Marigold rushed into the woods in search of a real bird's nest. Soon she saw one, high up in a tree. Huffing and puffing, Marigold climbed up to get it.

When she got to the nest, Marigold saw several lovely little pale blue eggs inside. "Splendid!" Marigold said. But the moment Marigold reached for the nest, the mother bird shrieked and dove at her. Marigold almost fell from the tree trying to protect her eyes.

After a few more tries, Marigold finally gave up trying to take the bird's nest. She climbed back down the tree and began to sob. But then she saw some white oval eggs lying in the sand at her feet.

"Some silly bird has placed her eggs right on the ground!" Marigold said aloud. She snatched them up and quickly fashioned a nest from some bent twigs and vines. She placed the nest on her hat and put the eggs inside it. Then she ran back to the fair.

Marigold hurried past the pie booth and the magic show. She pushed past children with candied apples and cotton candy. Finally, she saw the three ladies sitting at the hat-judging table.

Sure enough, Luella was turning her head this way and that, showing off the pink bow and the flowers and the dainty little bird's nest filled with glass eggs. The ladies were ooing and aahing all over the place, and they seemed about to award the prize to Luella.

"Wait!" cried Marigold, running breathlessly up to the table. "I want to enter my hat in the contest! See my beautiful hat? I have two pink bows while she has but one. I have two cloth canaries and she has but one. I have twelve bunches of flowers, but she has only six bunches. And see my bird's nest—it's filled with real eggs!"

"Eeeeeeek," cried one of the ladies at the judging table. She clasped her hands to her face.

"Oooooo," groaned the second lady at the table, looking as if she might faint.

"Ugh!" said the third lady, scrambling from the table and running away.

When Marigold took off her hat, she was horrified. Six baby snakes were hatching from the eggs and crawling from the nest! Marigold gasped and flung her hat so far that it landed in a meadow. The baby snakes all hurried home. A large crow found the hat and used it for her own nest.

And Luella won the prize for having the most beautiful hat at the fair.